The
SKY UNICORN

MORE MAGICAL RESCUES!

The Storm Dragon

COMING SOON:

The Baby Firebird
The Magic Fox

The Secret Rescuers

The
SKY UNICORN

By Paula Harrison

Illustrated by SOPHY WILLIAMS

ALADDIN

New York   London   Toronto   Sydney   New Delhi

ALADDIN

An imprint of Simon & Schuster Children's Publishing Division

1230 Avenue of the Americas, New York, New York 10020

First Aladdin paperback edition March 2017

Text copyright © 2015 by Paula Harrison

Illustrations copyright © 2015 by Sophy Williams

Originally published in the United Kingdom in 2015 by Nosy Crow Ltd

Published by arrangement with Nosy Crow

Also available in an Aladdin hardcover edition.

All rights reserved, including the right of reproduction in whole or in part in any form.

ALADDIN and related logo are registered trademarks of Simon & Schuster, Inc.

For information about special discounts for bulk purchases, please contact Simon & Schuster
Special Sales at 1-866-506-1949 or business@simonandschuster.com.

The Simon & Schuster Speakers Bureau can bring authors to your live event.
For more information or to book an event contact the Simon & Schuster Speakers Bureau
at 1-866-248-3049 or visit our website at www.simonspeakers.com.

Cover designed by Steve Scott

Interior designed by Tom Daly

The text of this book was set in ITC Clearface.

Manufactured in the United States of America 1017 OFF

2 4 6 8 10 9 7 5 3

Library of Congress Control Number 2016932244

ISBN 978-1-4814-7611-9 (hc)

ISBN 978-1-4814-7610-2 (pbk)

ISBN 978-1-4814-7612-6 (eBook)

Chapter One

✦ ⦂ ✦

The Snow-White Foal

Ava leaned over the side of the boat and let her fingers trail through the cool water. It was wonderful to sail along with the breeze tickling her cheek and ruffling her long black hair. She loved watching the ducks swim and seeing rabbits scampering along the sandy bank. The river ran all the way through the Emerald Plain, and there was so much wildlife to see.

Sometimes, if she was really lucky, Ava would catch sight of a magical creature. There were lots of amazing magical animals in the Kingdom of

Arramia, such as giant eagles with golden feathers, star wolves that sang, and even sky unicorns!

The river sparkled in the sunshine. Two planets, one green and one purple, hung in the cloudless sky.

Leaning out a bit farther, Ava watched the six boats following hers down the river. Each one had a large white sail and a cabin painted in bright red, blue, and green. Ava and her family were part of Mr. Inigo's Amazing Traveling Troupe. They sailed up and down the kingdom's lakes and rivers, stopping in every town to put on a show. Right now they were on their way to the town of Blyford on the shores of Misty Lake.

Ava smiled to herself. She couldn't wait for the next show. She was going to perform a new dance in the turquoise dress she was wearing. She'd been practicing for weeks!

"Ava, don't lean out too far," said her mother. "You don't want to fall in with that nice dress on!"

Ava moved back a little and smoothed the folds of the turquoise dress. It was made of a silky material that shimmered in the light. "Are we close to Misty Lake yet?"

"It's not far now," her mother replied. "I expect we'll look for a place to camp soon."

Her dad came out of the cabin and took hold of the main rope to pull in the sail. Then he fetched a small silver trumpet and blew a single note.

On the next boat Ava's three older brothers took down their sail. Then they blew a note on their own silver trumpet. This was how they sent messages down the line of boats. Soon all the sails were in, and the boats slowed down a little.

"There's Misty Lake—just beyond the bridge." Her dad pointed to a wooden bridge not far downstream. A mass of glittering water lay just beyond it.

"I can see it!" Ava made a graceful jump, raising her arms as if they were wings. Then she twirled around. They were moves from her new dance.

"Ava!" Her mother laughed. "Remember, no dancing on the boat. There isn't room!"

"Sorry, I forgot!" Ava stopped herself halfway through the spin.

The boat sailed around a bend in the river, and a towering hill came into view. Standing at the top was a pale shape that made Ava catch her breath.

It was a sky unicorn.

As Ava watched, more unicorns trotted over the brow of the hill, their snowy manes flowing in the breeze. With their beautiful white coats, golden horns, and brightly colored tails, they were the most beautiful animals she'd ever seen.

Ava felt as if butterflies were dancing inside her. She'd seen sky unicorns before, but never so many together. There must have been at least twenty of them! The tallest one at the front lifted its head, and its golden horn gleamed in the sunlight. Ava had heard stories about how sky unicorns could gallop into the air and race right through the clouds, but she'd never seen them do it. She watched them eagerly, but the magical animals showed no sign of leaving the hill.

"They're amazing, aren't they?" said her dad.

"Now, where did I put the spare mooring rope?"

"I wish they'd fly," sighed Ava. "If I could gallop through the sky, I'd do it all the time."

"Perhaps there's a foal," said her mother. "Unicorns will often stay on the ground if there's a foal, because the little ones can't fly until they're older. Now, I'd better help your dad find that rope." She hurried away.

The sky unicorns walked slowly down the hill to the river, close to Ava's boat. A little foal skipped to the front of the herd, its turquoise tail swishing happily. Then it bent its head to drink from the river. Ava was so excited she could hardly breathe. She'd never seen a unicorn foal before. Its legs were slender, and its soft coat was so white it almost glowed. It raised its head and looked at her with big dark eyes.

"Hello, I'm Ava!" she called softly.

The foal nodded its head and shook its snowy mane, almost as if it were saying hello back.

Just then a man dressed in armor and riding a horse appeared at the top of the hill. Ava guessed at once that he must be a knight. When he saw the unicorns, he shouted at two guards who were hurrying after him.

Then he drew his sword and rode down the slope toward the unicorns. "Stop, you horrible beasts!" he bellowed. "Stop in the name of the queen."

The unicorn foal jumped in fright, and its tail trembled.

Ava turned to her parents in alarm, but they'd both disappeared into the cabin.

The sky unicorns dashed along the riverbank, scared away by the knight's fierce shouting. He chased them, urging his horse to go faster. The sky unicorns quickened into a gallop. Racing along the riverbank, they dashed across the wooden bridge that spanned the river. Their hooves made a sound like thunder.

The knight urged his horse to go faster, but he couldn't match their speed. "How dare you!" he yelled. "Come back at once! All magical beasts are to be captured, by royal order." He called to his men, but they were slowed down by their heavy swords and shields.

Ava watched with wide eyes. Why would *anyone* want to chase a unicorn? The herd had almost reached the end of the bridge now. Soon they would be on the other side of the river. Ava smiled as she watched them gallop so quickly. Then her heart dropped.

Where was the foal?

Quickly she scanned the bridge and the river-bank. The foal had fallen over beside a bramble patch halfway to the bridge. It was trying to stand up again, but its leg was caught by a prickly branch.

"Mom, Dad, quick!" Ava called, but her parents didn't come out of the cabin. The boats behind theirs were hidden by the bend in the river and couldn't see what was happening.

Ava's heart thumped faster. The knight was riding toward the bridge with his sword in his hand. Any moment now he might notice the baby unicorn.

Ava ran to the back of the boat and turned the ship's wheel so that the boat drifted closer to the bank. Then, as soon as she was sure the water was shallow, she climbed onto the side of the boat and jumped in.

Chapter Two

⭐ ⚬⋅✳

The Noise in the Dark

Ava landed in the river with a splash. The water reached her waist, soaking through her turquoise dancing dress. It was freezing cold, but there was no time to think about that. The little unicorn needed her help!

The knight was still riding hard, with his guards running after him. Their eyes were fixed on the herd of unicorns on the bridge. None of them had spotted the unicorn foal by the bramble patch.

"Come on, Huster! Get a move on, Brinch!" bellowed the knight. "We're losing them."

The guards tried to run faster, their heavy shields bouncing against their sides. Making sure they weren't looking, Ava waded to the edge of the river and scrambled up the bank. The little unicorn shivered as she got closer.

She crouched down, glad that she was hidden from the knight and his guards by the tangle of bushes. "Don't worry!" she whispered to the foal. "I won't hurt you."

The foal gave a soft whinny and gazed at her with big dark eyes.

"What happened?" Ava stroked its snowy mane. "Are you stuck?" She gently checked its hooves and found the bramble caught round its leg.

The foal twitched nervously.

"It's all right," said Ava, carefully untangling the hoof. "There—all done!" The foal sprang to its feet and skipped around, tossing its head in delight.

Ava peeked over the bushes to check that the knight hadn't seen them. She sighed with relief when she saw the men crossing the bridge. But where had the unicorn herd gone? The knight and the guards reached the other side of the river and disappeared along the road leading to town. Ava spotted the sky-unicorn herd almost hidden behind a grove of trees near the water's edge.

"There's your herd!" Ava told the little unicorn, pointing to the opposite bank. "Can you find your way?"

The foal seemed to think it could. It brushed its nose against her hair and then skipped across the bridge and through the trees to join the herd again.

Ava smiled as she watched it. Then she hurried to the water's edge and waded back to the boat. Her muddy dress clung to her legs. Her mother would scold her for getting messy, but she didn't mind. She was so glad the foal was safe again.

Ava was relieved that everyone thought she'd just waded in the river for fun. Her mother and dad had been busy searching for the mooring rope in the cabin. The rest of the troupe had sailed round the bend in the river just as the knight had crossed the bridge. They'd been too busy staring at him to look at Ava. She was happy that her meeting with the unicorn foal was her special secret!

"Honestly, Ava!" scolded her mother. "What were you thinking, splashing around in your dancing dress? I don't think I'll be able to wash those mud stains out."

"Sorry, Mom!" Ava said meekly.

The seven boats that made up Mr. Inigo's Amazing Traveling Troupe sailed along to the bridge, where they tied up. Everyone disembarked and built a fire for cooking their dinner. They were going to have a stew made with freshly caught fish from the river.

The troupe relaxed around the campfire while the stew was cooking. Everyone was

16

there: the married acrobats, Monty and May; Ava's three older brothers, the juggling triplets; the Kittersons, who put on plays; Ruben Gribba, the magician; and the grown-up dancers, Floella and Daisy, with Daisy's four-year-old daughter, Lucy. Then there was Mr. Inigo, who sang opera music in his splendid, deep voice. Ava's parents didn't perform anymore, but they helped with all the costumes and sold tickets for the shows.

"This is an excellent place to stop for the night," said Mr. Inigo, twirling his long black mustache. "It's only a few minutes' walk into Blyford. Tomorrow we'll go into town to put up posters for our Grand Show!"

"I hope we'll all get a bit more money this time," grumbled Ruben the magician, stroking his long beard. "I hardly got any coins from that last place."

"The coins are always shared out fairly," said Ava's mother. "Perhaps you spent all yours too fast."

Ruben got up, muttering something about measly wages. "I'm going to collect firewood."

Ava stared across the river. Were the unicorns still sheltering among the trees on the other side? It was hard to see now that it was growing dark.

"We need some more herbs for the stew," said Ava's dad, stirring the huge pot. "Some mint and rosemary, I think."

"I'll get them!" said Ava quickly. "I won't be long." She took a lantern and hurried toward the bridge. She'd look for the unicorns while she collected the herbs. Maybe she'd even get to see the little foal again!

Her footsteps sounded loud on the wooden planks. She watched the river flowing slowly under the bridge into the huge lake beyond. When she reached the other side, she tiptoed through the trees into the little valley, where the sky unicorns had hidden.

They were still there. Some were grazing and others were resting. Their pale coats and manes shone in the twilight. The little foal was sleeping next to a larger unicorn that Ava guessed must be its mother. She gazed at them for a while, not wanting to get too close in case she alarmed them.

A movement near the trees made her turn round. A figure was creeping away from the unicorns toward the bridge. It was Ruben Gribba, the magician, with his thin face and long beard. Ava wondered if he wanted to see the unicorns again too, except he didn't seem like the sort of person who liked animals.

He wasn't carrying any firewood, either.

Ava watched the unicorns for a while. Then she realized it had got much darker and her dad needed herbs for the stew. She hurried away and picked some mint leaves growing close to the river.

She was about to cross the bridge when she heard a strange rushing sound in the air. She peered up into the darkness. What *was* that? It almost sounded like huge wings beating.

The noise grew louder, ending in a gigantic splash.

Ava went in the direction of the sound. Something pretty big must have landed in the water to make such a loud splash.

Then, to her surprise, she heard a girl's voice.

"Windrunner! Did you have to land in the river? I'm soaking wet!" A long string of growls answered her.

Ava raised her lantern, but she couldn't see very far. "Hello?" she said. "Is everyone all right?"

"Who's there?" the girl called back.

"I'm Ava, from Mr. Inigo's Traveling Troupe. Do you need help?" Ava peered into the darkness. She thought she could see two shapes near the water's edge. One of them seemed absolutely huge. There were more growls—quieter this time.

Ava clambered down the bank and then stopped short. A blond-haired girl was standing by the edge of the river, clutching a small cloth bag. Water dripped from her dress.

Right next to her, shaking water off its wings, was a huge green dragon.

Chapter Three

* ⋅∘※

The Magical Stone

Ava stared at the dragon. It coughed, and a little flame spurted out of its mouth. "Don't be scared. He's really friendly!" said the girl. "Are you all alone?"

"Um . . . yes, I am." Ava still couldn't take her eyes off the dragon. She'd seen the creatures flying in the distance before, but she'd never actually *met* one. It was enormous—nearly the size of her boat—and its skin was so scaly.

"You don't mind dragons, do you?" the girl asked eagerly.

"No, not at all!" Ava smiled. Now that she'd gotten over the surprise, it really was very exciting to be so close to a dragon. She wondered why the girl and the dragon were together. She'd never heard of dragons being friends with humans before.

The girl shaded her eyes from the light of Ava's lantern. "I'm Sophy, and this is my friend Windrunner, the storm dragon. We've flown for miles and miles to get here!" She clambered up the bank toward Ava but tripped on some rough ground and fell over.

The little cloth bag flew from her fingers, and a handful of stones fell out onto the grass. Sophy gasped and snatched up the bag again immediately.

"Are you all right? Here, I'll help." Ava set the lantern on the ground and began picking up the fallen stones. They were small—each one was no bigger than a strawberry. She held one close to the lantern to get a better look. It was gray and lumpy, and not very pretty at all.

Suddenly the stone glowed orange and felt hot against her skin. "Ouch!" She dropped it, afraid it would burn her fingers. "What's happening?"

"Wait!" breathed Sophy. "You'll see. . . ."

Ava's eyes widened as the rock blazed brighter and brighter. With a snap it broke in half, and the orange glow faded. Her fingers trembling, Ava picked up the two pieces of rock. Each one had a tiny hollow inside, filled with sparkling, emerald-green crystals.

"That's amazing!" whispered Ava.

"It's magic, and I can show you how it works!" Sophy smiled widely. "This is fantastic luck! I didn't think I'd find anyone so quickly."

Ava stared at the other girl, her mind whirling. She really wasn't sure what Sophy meant about finding someone. "This stone is magic? Really?" She looked down at the two pieces of rock in her hand. The green crystals glittered.

"Yes, really!" Sophy nodded vigorously. "I know it must seem strange . . . but you see, the same thing happened to me! This is a Speaking Stone. It lets you talk to magical animals. The queen threw out this bag of stones as if they were trash after the king died."

"She didn't know they were magical, then?"

"No, and she doesn't like magic anyway."
Sophy lifted a thread over her neck. "Your stone
will only work for you. See, I have one of my own!
Now I talk to magical animals all the time." She
showed Ava a stone
dangling on the
end of the thread.
It looked rough and

gray on the outside, like Ava's. Opening the stone, Sophy revealed a little cave of purple crystals.

"So I'll be able to talk to magical animals too?" Ava almost squeaked with excitement.

"Try it now!" Sophy grabbed Ava's hand. "Say something to Windrunner."

Ava faced the dragon and swallowed. "H-hello, Windrunner! I'm pleased to meet you."

Windrunner blinked his amber eyes and bowed his head. "Pleased to meet you, too. Any friend of Sophy's is a friend of the storm dragons!"

Ava gasped. It was just so strange hearing the growling noise from his mouth turn into words.

"You *see*!" Sophy was bouncing on her toes. "It's very lucky I found you. The stones only work for a few people, and I really need your help, because danger is coming. That's why I'm here!"

"What's the danger?" asked Ava.

"There's a knight at the royal castle who hates magical animals—a really horrible man! He's set out to destroy them, and we think he's on his way here right now. We've spent all day flying around looking for him, but we haven't seen him yet."

"I'm very tired from all the flying!" grunted Windrunner. "I will rest a little, Sophy." He blew warm breath on the ground and then settled down with his tail curled around his body.

Sophy and Ava climbed to the top of the riverbank, where the path led to the bridge.

Ava held the two pieces of her magical stone tightly. "But how did you make friends with a dragon?"

"I rescued his baby brother from the castle,"

explained Sophy. "I work there as a maid. That's how I know Sir Fitzroy; he's the knight I was telling you about—" She broke off as footsteps sounded on the bridge.

"Ava, is that you?" called her mother. "Are you all right? You've been gone such a long time that we wondered where you'd got to."

"I'm fine, Mom! Just a minute," Ava called back, before whispering to Sophy, "I'm sorry—I have to go. But I really want to help . . . and a knight rode past here today. He might be the one you mean."

Sophy nodded. "Meet me here—just underneath the bridge—at first light, and we'll work out what to do. Remember, your stone only works for you! Don't show it to anyone."

"Don't worry. I won't!" Ava smiled at her new friend before hurrying away across the bridge.

So many strange things had happened in one day. First she'd helped the unicorn foal, and then this girl—Sophy—had appeared from nowhere! Now she had a special stone that let her talk to magical animals, and *that* was the most amazing thing of all!

Chapter Four

* . ✳

The Town by the Lake

Ava found it hard to sleep that night. She stared up at the drawings of famous dancers pinned on the wall above her cabin bed. Usually the gentle movement of the water underneath the boat helped her sleep, but tonight her mind was full of sky unicorns and magical stones.

Just before dawn she got up and took the special stone from under her pillow. Ava fetched a thread from the sewing basket and tied the two pieces together. She made the thread into a necklace and hung it round her neck as Sophy did. The stone was hidden beneath her dress where no one would see it.

Then she tiptoed out of the cabin and climbed to shore. Feeling a little shy, she crossed the bridge to find Sophy and Windrunner.

Sophy was already waiting for her. "Are those your boats?" She pointed across the river.

"Yes, we travel along the rivers and lakes putting on shows in each town." Ava forgot her shyness as she told Sophy all about the different acts in their show.

Sophy was especially interested in Ava's dancing. Then she told Ava about life in the castle and her troubles with the wicked knight Sir Fitzroy.

Ava nodded. "He sounds just like the knight I saw yesterday." And she explained to Sophy how he'd chased the sky unicorns before galloping toward Blyford.

Sophy's cheeks flushed. "Horrible man! If he took the path to town, we should follow him and see if we can find out what his plan is."

Windrunner lumbered up the riverbank and yawned, showing rows of glistening teeth. Then he shook his tail and stretched his leathery wings. "If you are venturing into the human town, then I must leave you for now, dear Sophy," he said. "I'll scare the townspeople if I fly too close to their houses. Send a golden songbird to find me when you need me again."

"Thanks, Windrunner." Sophy hugged him.

The big green dragon launched into the air and flew away across Misty Lake. Ava watched him soar upward, amazed at how fast he could fly. She noticed how the wind gusted and the clouds swirled as the dragon flew away.

Sophy's stomach rumbled. "I didn't realize I was so hungry."

"I'll bring us some breakfast," said Ava. "And I'll fetch Mr. Inigo's show posters. Pinning them up gives me a good reason for going to town."

Quickly Ava fetched some blueberry scones and a handful of the posters. The girls sat on a tree stump and munched their breakfast.

"Thanks, Ava!" Sophy beamed. "These are delicious."

Ava smiled back a little shyly. There was something she really wanted to ask. She just hoped

Sophy wouldn't mind. "Do you think . . . do we have time to look at the sky unicorns before we go to town?"

Sophy glanced at the sun rising in the sky. "I'd love to see them too. We can be quick, can't we?"

Ava nodded eagerly. "They're in a hidden valley not very far away—I'll show you!" She led Sophy away from the bridge. They crept through the trees and down the slope into the little dell that Ava had visited the evening before.

Many of the unicorns were awake and grazing quietly. They raised their heads as the girls tiptoed closer, and their golden horns gleamed in the sunlight. Then, when they saw that it was Ava and Sophy, they went back to nibbling the grass again.

"Aren't they beautiful?" whispered Sophy, her blue eyes shining. "I guess you've seen sky unicorns before, but I've lived in the castle my whole life. I've seen plenty of royal banquets and golden crowns, but I've never seen anything as amazing as these creatures!"

"I never saw them close up till yesterday," said Ava. "Look, there's the little foal!"

The baby unicorn left its mother and gamboled around the dell, flicking its little tail. Ava crouched down and held out her hand. The foal tossed its snowy mane and gazed at her. Then, at last, it trotted up and gently nibbled her fingers.

Ava's heart leaped. She'd hardly dared hope that she would get so close to it again, and now the magical stone gave her the chance to talk to it too!

She swallowed. "Hello, my name's Ava. Don't be afraid—I have a magical stone that lets me talk to you."

The foal looked startled and took a few steps back. Then it crept closer again. "My name's Clover," he said in a soft, high whinny. "Thank you for helping me yesterday!"

"You're welcome!" Ava smiled.

Clover danced forward and nibbled at Ava's hair before galloping off around the valley again.

"What a sweet little foal," said Sophy. "Come on, let's go into town and see if Sir Fitzroy is there. I'm determined that he won't have the chance to harm any magical creatures."

The girls left the tiny hidden valley and followed the path to town. Blyford was a large place with bustling streets and a town square in the middle.

Sophy gazed round. "I've never been to a town this big before! You must be used to all this because of traveling around on the boat. You live an amazing life!"

"You live in the royal castle!" said Ava. "That's pretty awesome!"

"Well, I do like polishing the queen's tiaras," said Sophy, laughing.

Ava giggled too. She couldn't help liking Sophy. She was so chatty and had a warm smile. There were so many questions she wanted to ask her, like how many tiaras did the queen have? And how had Sophy rescued the little dragon? And when Sophy was flying on Windrunner's back, wasn't she afraid of falling off?

She was just wondering what to ask first when she saw a man in silver armor on the other side of the town square. "That's the man who chased the unicorns!" she said to Sophy. "Is he your horrible knight?"

Sophy shivered. "Yes, that's Sir Fitzroy. I wonder what he's up to."

The girls crossed the square, weaving in and out between the fruit sellers and stalls full of shoes and hats. A tall lady dressed in a dark red cloak came out of a grand building and walked down the steps to shake the knight's hand.

"That's the leader of Blyford walking out of the town hall," muttered Ava. "Her name's Dame Gibson."

Ava and Sophy edged closer to the steps and then stopped to look at a hat stall. They pretended they were interested in buying a purple hat. It gave them the chance to listen to Sir Fitzroy's conversation.

"Greetings, Sir Fitzroy," said Dame Gibson. "We haven't seen you in Blyford for many years. What brings you to our town?"

"I'm hunting down every magical beast in this kingdom," snarled Sir Fitzroy. "Her Majesty,

Queen Viola, was nearly killed by a dragon attack on her own castle two days ago. It's time we sorted out these disgusting creatures once and for all."

Chapter Five

⋆ ⦂⁛※

Mr. Inigo's Show Begins

Ava glanced over her shoulder at Sir Fitzroy, who was still talking to the town leader. "Was there really a dragon attack?" she murmured to Sophy.

"No!" Sophy whispered back. "There was one poor baby dragon who wanted to go home."

Dame Gibson shook her head. "I'm shocked, Sir Fitzroy! Here in Blyford we've always loved magical animals. Many creatures such as sky unicorns roam the Emerald Plain. I can't believe they deserve such harsh treatment."

"You can say what you like, but you'll have to obey royal orders like everyone else," growled Sir Fitzroy, unrolling a scroll of paper with the mark of a crown. "Now, where do these sky unicorns live? I saw them yesterday, but the wretched things sneaked away. I command you to show me where they are."

Dame Gibson shook her head. "I'm afraid I can't. People say that the sky unicorns have favorite places where they like to graze, but there are lots of little valleys on the Emerald

Plain. They could be anywhere!"

Someone coughed just behind Ava. She turned her head and thought she recognized the man behind her, but he disappeared into the crowd before she could be sure.

"Look, Ava!" Sophy nudged her. "Is that your traveling troupe?"

A murmur of excitement ran through the town square as Mr. Inigo swept in, wearing the multicolored patchwork cloak that he put on for each show. Behind him were the acrobats, Ava's brothers the jugglers, and the dancers Floella and Daisy.

Ava suddenly remembered that she was supposed to have put up posters for the show. She quickly ran to pin them on the nearby walls.

"Roll up! Roll up!" called Mr. Inigo, twirling his mustache. "Come and see a few acts from our show for free. Then buy tickets for our spectacular Grand Show tonight!"

"Ava, we need you." Ava's brother Rick tapped her shoulder. "Mr. Inigo's decided to set up right here and show the crowd a few of our acts so that they buy tickets for tonight. We need you to dance."

"All right, then!" Ava felt a fizzing in her tummy. Dancing in front of a crowd was always exciting and a little bit scary.

"I'll watch you—good luck!" said Sophy.

The acrobats, Monty and May, laid out dancing mats and tied a ribbon around eight poles to keep the performance area clear. The crowd pressed forward, eager to see.

"Ava!" Floella dashed over and handed Ava her dance shoes. "Start with your freestyle routine and finish with the ballet. Mr. Inigo will play the music for you."

"Thanks, Floella." Ava put on her dance shoes and smoothed her long, dark hair.

Mr. Inigo held up his hands for silence. "And first I'd like to introduce one of our youngest and best dancers. Please give a round of applause for the Astounding . . . the Amazing . . . the Awesome Ava!"

The crowd clapped wildly. Ava blushed and got into her starting position with her legs straight and her arms high above her head. Her heart was racing as Mr. Inigo began to play the tune on his violin.

As soon as she started to dance, Ava forgot to be nervous. She sometimes wondered how she could dance in front of a crowd when she often felt so shy. The music swirling round her seemed to set her free. She leaped and spun to the beat, and the crowd began to clap in time with the music.

Ava finished her first dance and dropped a curtsy, blushing again at the cheers from the townspeople.

Sophy was standing right at the front. "Well done, Ava!" she called. "You were great!"

Mr. Inigo twirled his mustache again and then struck up a slower melody. This was the music for Ava's favorite ballet. Pointing her toes, she moved to the music and leaped gracefully across the floor. Then she swayed and twirled before performing a beautiful arabesque.

As she turned to repeat her movements, something caught her eye. The knight, Sir Fitzroy, was still standing on the steps. He was frowning as if he wasn't enjoying the performance at all. Then a figure slipped out of the crowd and joined him.

Ruben Gribba, the magician, muttered in Sir Fitzroy's ear. A nasty smile spread across the knight's face, which turned Ava's heart cold. The movement of the dance took her in the other direction. When she turned back again, Sir Fitzroy was giving Ruben a handful of gold coins. Then the two men walked down the steps together and disappeared behind the crowd.

Ava carried on dancing, but an icy dread poured through her. What had Ruben done? She pictured him the evening before, watching the unicorns grazing in their hidden valley. Was it possible he'd told the knight where to find them? She wanted to run after the two men, but she was in the middle of a dance and everyone was watching. What was she supposed to do?

She kept on going till the end and tried to smile as the crowd applauded her. Then, when Mr. Inigo announced the next act, she slipped away and found Sophy. "Quickly!" she gasped. "The knight's gone! I think Ruben told him where to find the sky unicorns."

"Who's Ruben?" said Sophy.

"He belongs to our troupe. He was talking to

Sir Fitzroy. Then they both disappeared really fast."

The girls struggled to get through the crowd. They reached the edge of the square, but for a moment Ava couldn't remember which street to follow. At last she recognized the right one, and the girls ran until their legs ached. They stopped where the houses ended, trying to catch their breath.

"It'll take us too long to get back to the bridge," said Sophy. "If Sir Fitzroy's riding his horse, he could be there already!"

Ava looked round desperately. She pictured Clover galloping round the hidden valley, his turquoise tail flying. She couldn't let Sir Fitzroy hurt him. There had to be a way to get there faster.

They were close to the waterfront where the boats were moored. Ava noticed her brothers' boat tied to the jetty. They must have sailed up here with the dancing mats and other equipment.

"We'll catch up with them if we go by boat," she told Sophy. "This one belongs to my brothers. Come on, let's go!"

Sophy climbed aboard while Ava untied the mooring rope. Then they each took an oar and rowed as hard as they could. Ava wished she could have asked her family for help, but if Sir Fitzroy discovered they'd gone against royal orders, they'd all be in terrible trouble. She and Sophy would have to help the sky unicorns without anyone finding out.

The wind whistled across the lake, whipping up little waves. After resting her oar, Ava put up the sail, and the boat speeded up at once. They glided up the lake toward the river just as Sir Fitzroy and Ruben Gribba rode onto the bridge. The knight got off his horse and took out a small telescope to peer closely at the riverbank. Ruben pointed in the direction of the hidden valley, and Sir Fitzroy mounted his horse again before they rode off together.

"Now what?" said Sophy. "Shall we row to shore?"

Ava's forehead creased. "We're still going to be too late. We have to let the unicorns know they're in danger!"

She dived into the cabin and rummaged under her brother's things. She threw juggling sticks and bean bags aside. She flung odd socks and orange peels out of her way. Then she found what she wanted: a gleam of silver under all the mess.

"Found it!" She drew out a large silver trumpet. "We're going to warn the sky unicorns without anyone ever knowing it was us."

Chapter Six

★ ◆ ∗

The Silver Trumpet

Will it work?" Sophy eyed the trumpet doubtfully.

"It makes a really horrible noise every time I

try to play it. I'm sure it would scare any animal!

There might be some drums in there too. See if you can find them." Ava dashed back to the deck.

The boat had glided closer to the bridge, with its narrowly spaced pillars.

"Sophy!" called Ava. "Can you help me with the sail? We'll have to take it down to get under the bridge."

"Sure!" Sophy ran out carrying a red-and-white drum and two drumsticks. "What do I need to do?"

Ava showed her which rope lowered the mainsail. Sophy put down the drum, and together they heaved and heaved until the tall white sail came down. Then they tied the rope firmly in place.

"To the oars!" said Ava.

They had to work the oars hard, as they were rowing against the current. Luckily, the water was calm and the boat kept steady. Pulling hard, they rowed under the bridge and out the other side. Then they turned the boat toward the shore where the unicorn's hidden valley met the water's edge.

Glimpses of white coats and golden horns could be seen between the trees. Ava felt excitement rising inside her. The sky unicorns were still there. She and Sophy had made it in time. Two unicorns with purple tails raised their heads as the boat zoomed into view.

"Run away!" Sophy called to the creatures. "Danger's coming!" But the wind whipped the words from her mouth, and the unicorns were too far away to understand.

Ava lifted the silver trumpet to her lips. She had to get this right. It had to be a really loud sound to scare the sky unicorns away. She took a deep breath, then blew into the instrument.

All that came out was a funny blowing noise, like an elephant with a cold. "Try again!" urged Sophy. "Maybe you need to blow harder."

Ava pushed her dark hair out of her eyes and blew again. This time she made a deep, harsh sound. The unicorns looked up, their tails swishing anxiously, but they didn't run away.

Ava took a huge breath and blew again.

This time she made a noise so horrible that Sophy put her hands over her ears. "That sounds *totally* awful!" she shouted over the din. "I'll join in with the drum." She grabbed the drum and started banging it very fast.

The sky unicorns sprang away, galloping across the little valley.

"Look, they're leaving!" cried Sophy. "Well done, Ava. That noise was terrible."

Ava beamed as she watched the sky unicorns disappearing through the trees. Then she saw a shadow moving on the other side of the valley. She ducked down behind a big coil of rope, pulling Sophy with her.

Sir Fitzroy marched down the steep slope, scowling deeply. He turned to shout something, but the girls were too far away to hear what it was.

"As soon as he's gone, we'll row back under the bridge," said Ava, and Sophy nodded.

Sir Fitzroy strode up and down the hidden valley a few times. Ava noticed him staring over at the boat, but she knew that she and Sophy couldn't be seen. She hoped that the knight would give up on finding the sky unicorns. The Emerald Plain was a huge place stretching hundreds of miles. If the unicorns were out of sight, he'd never find them.

The gentle movement of the river swept the boat along, and the valley started to disappear from view. Ava got ready to leap for the oars as soon as she had the chance. She glanced at the hidden valley one more time and gasped in horror.

Ruben, the magician, prowled down the slope to join Sir Fitzroy. He was holding a creature tightly round its middle. The little animal was wriggling its legs, but Ruben wouldn't let go. It had a snow-white coat and a turquoise tail.

Clover had been captured.

"No!" gasped Ava. "Not Clover!"

"Poor little thing!" cried Sophy. "He must have been slower to gallop away than the others."

Ava leaned out, desperately trying to see what was happening, but the river swept the boat on. The men and the little unicorn foal disappeared from sight.

Tears pricked Ava's eyes. "This is awful! How could Ruben be so mean? Clover's only a baby unicorn."

Sophy's cheeks flushed with anger. "They're both very bad men. What shall we do? Row the boat to shore right here and steal Clover back?"

Ava bit her lip. "That could be tricky. They're much bigger than we are! Let's follow them, and then we can work out a plan."

They rowed over to the riverbank and tied the boat up next to the bridge. Sneaking through the bushes, they saw the men just as they were tying a rope around Clover's neck. Ruben Gribba mounted his horse. Sir Fitzroy also climbed into his saddle, and they cantered toward Blyford, while the little unicorn was pulled along behind.

"He's taking Clover back to town," whispered Ava. "Maybe he's hoping to use Clover to lure the other unicorns into danger."

Sophy nodded. "That's exactly the kind of thing Sir Fitzroy would do."

The girls followed at a safe distance. Ava thought of how Clover had gamboled across the grass that morning with his white mane flying. Her heart ached to see him being dragged along

behind a horse with a rope around his neck. His head drooped, and he stumbled as they reached town, but Sir Fitzroy only shouted at him and jerked the rope.

They stopped outside an inn called the Rotten Cauliflower. Instantly Sir Fitzroy's guards rushed up to him. The knight yelled some orders, and one of the men took the horse to the stables while the other led the foal inside. Then Sir Fitzroy gave more silver coins to Ruben, who walked away, stroking his beard and looking very pleased with himself.

Ava felt a lump in her throat as she watched Clover being led away. She couldn't believe Ruben had been so heartless and told the knight about the unicorns' hiding place for a few coins. Worst of all, he'd taken Clover from his family. She'd never thought he would be so mean.

"Sir Fitzroy must be staying here tonight," she said to Sophy. "We'll have to get inside to rescue Clover."

"How?" Sophy whispered back. "They'll know as soon as they see us that we're not supposed to be there."

Ava thought hard. "I know a way we can do it. We'll just need to borrow a few things. Let's go—we haven't got much time!"

Chapter Seven

✦ ∴ ✱

The Two Page Boys

Ava rushed down the street to the town square, with Sophy close behind her. She was glad to see that Floella and Daisy were still there, packing the dancing costumes into a small wagon.

"Hello, Ava!" said Floella cheerfully. "I meant to tell you how good your dancing was today, but I couldn't see you after the show."

"Thank you!" Ava would normally have been delighted to be praised by Floella, who'd taught her every dance step she knew. But right now all she could think about was rescuing Clover. "Sophy and I left the square after I danced," she admitted. "And I need to ask you a favor."

Floella looked at her with wise brown eyes. "Go on! What is it?"

Ava put on her most pleading expression. "We need to borrow the two page-boy costumes. It's for a . . . sort of prank. Please, can we?"

Floella jerked her head toward the wagon. "I'm afraid those are right at the bottom of the costume pile."

"Don't worry! I'll get them without messing anything up." Ava climbed into the wagon and slid through the layers of shoes and dresses and cloaks. She came out with two page-boy coats in velvety dark red with gold buttons, two pairs of black trousers, and two dark red caps.

"Don't tear them!" said Floella with a pretend scowl. "We won't!" said Ava and Sophy together.

On the way back to the inn, they bought a piece of parchment paper from one of the market stalls and rolled it up into a scroll shape. It didn't look perfect, Ava thought, but it would have to do.

They changed into their costumes in an empty part of the stables. They hid their other clothes behind a bale of hay.

Ava tucked her long, dark hair under the velvet cap and turned to look at Sophy, who was also dressed in the dark red uniform. "You look funny!"

Sophy grinned. "So do you! And what's the scroll of paper for?"

"It's a fake message from the queen. It should be enough to get us inside, at least."

Sophy's smile was replaced by an anxious frown. "Are you sure this will work? I'm not really use to disguises and pretending to be someone else."

"Don't worry! We've got actors in our troupe, and I've watched them put on plays lots of times," said Ava, pulling her cap low. "Just follow my lead." Her stomach tumbled as they left the stables, but she tried to ignore it. Clover was depending on her, and she wasn't going to let him down.

The girls marched up to the inn and rapped on the door. One of Sir Fitzroy's guards opened it. "You can't come in," he said roughly. "The whole inn is reserved for my master, and no one else—"

"We have a message for Sir Fitzroy from the queen," interrupted Ava, showing him the scroll of paper. "So you'd better let us through."

The guard stared at them for a moment. Ava kept her eyes down, crossing her fingers that they looked like page boys.

"He's upstairs having dinner," the guard said at last. "It's the second door on the left."

"Thank you!" Ava marched in and climbed the stairs, with Sophy close behind her. Luckily, the guard didn't follow them.

"There he is!" whispered Sophy.

The door to Sir Fitzroy's room was open a little. They could see him sitting at the table, his plate piled high with food. He was talking to the second guard. "So tomorrow we'll find out what makes the sky unicorn so *magical*." He said this last word as if it were disgusting. "Then we'll use the little beast to capture the rest of them."

Ava's heart sank. There was no time to lose! But where had they put Clover?

Tiptoeing along the corridor, she listened at each door. There was no noise behind any of them. Then she heard a faint crying coming from the end of the passage, where the stairway led up to the next floor.

Beckoning to Sophy, she hurried up the steps. It was dark at the top, and it took a few moments for her eyes to get used to the dim light. The crying sounded louder. Following the noise, Ava ran to the last room and pushed open the door.

Clover was trapped inside a small metal cage that stood on the bare floor. "I want my mummy," he sobbed. "It's horrible up here. I'm hungry!"

Ava dashed over to the cage. "Shh! Don't cry!" she begged. "It's me—Ava!"

The little foal stopped crying in surprise and whinnied, "Ava! You look different! What are you doing here?"

"We've come to rescue you, of course!" Ava told him. "Oh, Clover! I'm sorry you got

caught. Sir Fitzroy is such a horrible man!"

"Ava, I'll keep a lookout," said Sophy, pulling the door closed. "I'll knock if anyone comes."

"You really came to help me?" said Clover, starting to cheer up. "And you speak Sky Unicorn, too!"

"Do you remember the stone I showed you?" Ava pulled out the stone, which was hidden under her costume. "I can talk to you because of this. It has magic inside it."

"Like me!" said Clover eagerly. "I have magic inside me."

Ava smiled. "Just like you. Now, how does this cage open?" She studied the cage but couldn't see a lock or a key. At last she found a little catch on one side, but it wouldn't open. Curling her fingers through the bars, she tugged harder. The catch pinged open. A sharp metal point on

72

the end of the catch scraped across her finger and cut her skin.

"Ouch!" Ava looked at the cut. "Never mind! At least now you can come out of this awful cage."

Clover stepped free from the metal bars and flicked his tail in delight. Then he bent his little head close to Ava's hand. "Let me help you, Ava! This is our secret magic. We never show it to anybody, but I will share it with you!"

Ava watched in astonishment as the little unicorn bent his golden horn to touch her finger. Slowly the cut on her hand healed until it looked as if it had never been there at all.

"That's amazing!" breathed Ava. "Thank you."

"You're welcome." Clover gently nibbled her hair.

Ava threw her arms around him, and his snowy coat felt soft against her cheek. Then she

let go and sprang up. "Now we *must* get you out of here."

There was a quiet rapping on the door. Ava froze. That was Sophy's signal to say that someone was coming.

Creeping to the door, Ava heard a man's voice and footsteps on the stairs. Someone was climbing the steps, and it could be Sir Fitzroy. How would they get Clover to safety now?

Chapter Eight

✦ ⁖ ✲

Clover Takes a Leap

Ava's mind whirled. What should she do? Try to hide Clover under her jacket? He was far too big for that.

There was nothing in the room that would help her either—just a table and a chair. She ran to the window and swung it open. The streets of Blyford were far below. The sun had set now, and people were lighting the lamps.

An idea leaped to the front of her mind. "Clover!" she said eagerly. "I know sky unicorns learn to fly—can you do that yet?"

Clover shook his head sadly. "I'm too young to learn. My mom told me I can start flying when I'm older."

The footsteps outside drew nearer.

"What are you doing here, boy?" Sir Fitzroy's voice could be heard outside the door. "You must be up to no good if you're hanging around in the dark."

"I was just looking for the right room, sir," replied Sophy. "I came here with the other page boy to deliver a letter, but we . . . got a bit lost."

Clover began shivering at the sound of the knight's voice. Ava knelt down and put her arms round the foal's neck. "Clover," she whispered. "Would you try to fly? Just for me?"

Clover nodded. Then he took a few steps backward—a look of concentration on his little face. Ava smiled in encouragement, but her stomach lurched as she heard the knight speaking outside the door again.

"What are you talking about?" Sir Fitzroy snapped at Sophy. "I haven't seen any letter."

Clover cantered into the middle of the room and began galloping in circles, faster

and faster. The air sparkled around his hooves. Ava moved over to give him more space, but just as she started to feel hopeful, the little foal stopped.

His head drooped. "It's not working, Ava! I'm not flying."

Ava bit her lip. She could hear Sophy still

talking to Sir Fitzroy outside the door. Her friend was starting to sound desperate.

"What's going on in there? Stand aside, boy!" barked Sir Fitzroy.

"I know you can do it, Clover!" whispered Ava. "Think of your family flying. Remember the magic inside you!"

Clover cantered a little but then stopped again. "I don't know! What if I really can't do it?"

"Please, Clover!" cried Ava, not caring anymore if Sir Fitzroy heard her. "I believe in you!"

The little foal tossed his mane and began galloping round and round again. This time his hooves sparkled more brightly, as if they were sprinkled with stardust. Then, with one joyful leap, he sprang into the air and galloped right across the room without his hooves touching the floor.

"Fly, Clover! Fly!" cheered Ava.

Clover gave an excited whinny and cantered straight out the window.

The door wrenched open, and Sir Fitzroy marched over to the empty cage. "Where's the beast? Wicked boy, you've ruined my plan!"

Ava was barely listening. Leaning out the window, she watched Clover dash away into the night sky. He looked so beautiful, galloping beneath the stars. His white mane and turquoise tail lifted in the breeze, and a silvery trail sparkled where his hooves had been.

Ava's heart danced as she watched him. Then she frowned a little as he dipped lower. Was Clover all right? Was flying too hard for him?

Sir Fitzroy had finally worked out where Clover had gone. He pushed Ava aside in fury. "Sneaky animal!" he growled.

Ava saw Sophy beckoning from the doorway. She crept after her friend, glad that the knight was too busy glaring out the window to notice them escaping. They raced down two flights of stairs and out into the street.

Sophy ran to grab their clothes from the stables. "Clover's doing so well!" she said breathlessly.

"He's very brave, but it's the first time he's ever tried to fly." Ava stared upward, trying to spot the little unicorn. "What if he gets tired? He could hurt himself if he crashes into a rooftop."

"There he is!" Sophy pointed, and the girls began to run. There were shouts behind them as the guards gave chase.

The girls ran faster, dodging through streets and round corners. Clover cantered through the air, but his hooves dipped lower and lower.

Ava was certain he was getting tired. Surely they would reach the edge of town soon. Then Clover could land safely.

A few people stopped on the street to gaze up at the unicorn dashing through the night sky. They murmured in wonder at the glittering trail left behind by his hooves.

At last Ava and Sophy could see the edge of the town. Clover plunged lower, and the girls ran to meet him.

"Careful, Clover!" called Ava. "Go steady!"

"I'm falling!" whinnied the foal.

Stretching out her hands, Ava ran beneath him. He bumped down into her arms, knocking them both to the ground.

Ava giggled. "Clover, you're squashing me, and your tail is tickling my nose!"

Sophy helped them both up. "Are you all right?"

"Yes, I'm fine," said Ava. "Are you okay, Clover?"

The little unicorn danced around, with his ears pricked up and his tail swishing. "I flew! Did you see me? I really flew!"

"We saw you, and we're really

proud of you!" Sophy patted his snowy coat.

Ava cast a quick look behind her. "We need to keep going. Then we'll find a way to get you back to your herd, Clover."

Together they ran past the last few houses and the lakeside jetty. Then Ava found a place for them to hide behind a clump of bushes. Sir Fitzroy's guards ran by. The men searched the path and peered at the lake, but after a few minutes they gave up and went back into town.

Sophy peeked out. "They've gone at last!"

Clover gave a whinny of delight and jumped out of the bushes.

Ava laughed and hugged him. "You were very brave," she told him. "Flying for the very first time must have been really scary."

Clover nuzzled her shoulder. "It was at first, but you helped me." He gamboled up to Sophy and nuzzled her shoulder too. "Now I am Clover the Fabulous Flying Foal!"

Chapter Nine

* • *

The Grand Show

When they reached the bridge, Ava and Sophy changed back into their normal clothes, and they all stopped for a rest. Clover sat quietly on the grass, looking tired after all the excitement.

"Why don't we get Windrunner to help us search for the unicorn herd?" suggested Sophy. "He'll take us up into the air. It'll be so much easier to find them."

"Good idea," said Ava. "The Emerald Plain is such a huge place. We might get lost in the dark."

Sophy called a golden songbird by whistling a special tune that Windrunner the dragon had taught her. She explained to Ava that the songbirds carried messages for the other magical animals. Soon one of the golden birds heard her call. It flew down to perch on her hand and looked at her with bright black eyes.

"Please, could you ask Windrunner the storm dragon to meet me here?" asked Sophy.

"Of course!" The bird stretched its golden feathers and swooped away.

"It'll probably take Windrunner a while to fly here," said Sophy.

"You both stay here and I'll fetch us something to eat." Ava sprang to her feet and picked up the page-boy costumes.

"Yes, please! I am very hungry," said Clover, resting his head on Sophy's lap.

Ava crossed the bridge and hurried back to camp. She was a little worried that she would be asked to explain exactly what she'd been doing all day. She knew her family would love Clover, but she certainly didn't want to get them into trouble with Sir Fitzroy if he came asking questions the next day. Also, she knew that the troupe would be getting ready for the Grand Show later that evening.

When she reached the camp, she was surprised to find the troupe gathered round the fire. Ava's triplet brothers were arguing with an angry-looking Ruben. Ava frowned. She couldn't forget how nasty Ruben had been to poor Clover.

"I tell you I didn't take your boat!" said Ruben furiously.

"It must have been you," said Joe.

"You disappeared for ages this morning," said Ben. "And you came back looking guilty," added Rick.

"It wasn't me!" snapped Ruben.

"Then why was it tied up by the bridge instead of where we left it in town?" asked Joe.

Ava gasped. She was the one who had borrowed her brothers' boat. She was just about to own up when Ruben burst out, "I tell you, it wasn't me! I was busy showing that knight where the sky unicorns were hiding because . . ." He trailed off, suddenly aware of everyone frowning at him. "I just did it to be helpful."

"You did it for the money!" Ava burst out. "I saw the knight handing you some coins afterward."

"Well, so what if you did?" sneered Ruben. "It's none of your business anyway."

"You didn't care about the unicorns at all!" Ava's cheeks went bright red. "And you didn't care about the little foal you took away from his mother."

"Is this true, Ava?" Her mother got up and took her daughter's hand.

Ava nodded. "I was with my new friend, Sophy. We both saw what he did."

Ava's mother rounded

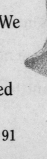

on Ruben. "You should be ashamed of yourself!"

Ruben's eyes glittered. "I deserved that money!" He pointed at Ava. "And she is just a horrible little sneak!"

All the members of the troupe started talking loudly at once. "Take that back!" Ava's brothers yelled at Ruben.

"Magical animals should never be treated so cruelly," said Floella, shaking her head.

Mr. Inigo rose and held up his hand for silence. "Ruben, it's clear that you do not deny what Ava has said. I'm afraid there's no place in our troupe for someone who has abandoned what's right for the sake of money."

"B-But . . . ," sputtered Ruben.

"You must go," said Mr. Inigo, and the other members of the troupe nodded in agreement.

"Fine! I don't want to stay with you anyway."

Ruben glared round at all of them before marching away to pack his things.

Ava put the page-boy costumes back where they belonged. Then she fetched some small fruit pies, and some lettuce and carrots for Clover, and ran back to the other side of the river.

"Yum!" Clover bounded up to Ava and tugged the vegetables from her hands.

"Thanks, Ava. This is delicious!" said Sophy, tasting a fruit pie. "The songbird came back while you were gone. Windrunner will be here at dawn. We can rest till then."

"Actually, it's the Grand Show tonight. I nearly

forgot because I was thinking so hard about rescuing Clover," explained Ava. "I should really go and dance. I don't want to let the troupe down."

"Have a wonderful time!" said Sophy. "We'll be fine here. Won't we, Clover?" Clover nodded as he chomped on another carrot.

Mr. Inigo's Amazing Traveling Troupe put on a spectacular show that night. Ava's brothers juggled with glowing sticks. Monty and May did rows of somersaults until the crowd gasped and clapped. Then Floella and Daisy performed a ribbon dance, twirling and spinning their long purple ribbons.

Ava joined the two grown-up dancers for their final number. Her pale blue dress floated around her as she leaped and spun. Then she performed a beautiful ballet by herself. As the music played, she lifted her arms and pointed her toes, enjoying every step. The crowd clapped loudly when she finished, and they called for an encore. Ava blushed and made another curtsy. She was so happy they'd loved her dancing!

Finally Monty and May climbed the tall towers that had been put up on either side of the arena. Hanging from their trapezes, they began to glide through the air. Ava always loved watching their act. It was awesome seeing them soar so high.

Suddenly her heart fluttered. She would be riding on a dragon for the very first time tonight. The acrobats were flying high on their trapezes, but she would be going even higher!

Chapter Ten

* .:*

Ava's First Flight

After the show was over, and all the costumes and equipment were packed away, Ava told her mother and father about her plan.

"Sophy and I are going to take Clover, the unicorn foal, back to his herd," she said. "We're going to . . . um . . . ride on a dragon to get there!" She crossed her fingers, hoping her parents wouldn't say she wasn't allowed.

"You're old enough to be sensible, Ava," said her mother. "As long as you let us know where you are and remember to thank the dragon."

"Your grandmother used to say she'd once ridden a dragon," said her dad. "She was an acrobat. I think she liked the excitement of flying through the sky."

Ava wondered whether she was going to like flying too. Her insides felt wobbly as she kissed her parents and went to find Sophy and Clover.

They waited a long time by the bridge. At last, just as the color of dawn began creeping into the sky, the sound of wingbeats filled the air.

Sophy leaped up at once. "Windrunner, is that you?"

The noise grew louder, and swirls of wind lifted the girls' hair. Windrunner landed in the river with an enormous splash. He paddled to the edge, climbed out, and shook the water off his huge, leathery wings. The girls stood back so they wouldn't get soaked.

"Hello, Sophy! Hello, Ava!" Windrunner looked at Clover with kind amber eyes. "Hello, little unicorn."

"Hello, Windrunner," said Ava. "It's great to see you."

Sophy ran up to give the dragon a hug. "Thank you for coming back."

Windrunner bowed his head. "Where to now, Sophy?"

"We're taking this foal back to the sky unicorn herd," Sophy told him.

Windrunner made Sophy stand back before giving out a long, fiery breath to dry off his wet scales. "Climb on!"

Sophy and Ava scrambled on. Clover didn't want to at first, but Sophy explained that it might be too far for him to fly. He found it hard to balance on Windrunner's back, but the girls helped him up, and soon they were all sitting down safely. Ava's heart thumped as she held on tight.

With a massive leap Windrunner took off. He soared high above the river before swooping down till they almost touched the water. Then he rose high again, taking them up and up until Ava thought she could almost touch the clouds.

The Emerald Plain rolled
past below them. Ava gazed at
the long, curving shape of the river that she was
so used to sailing along. It was strange to see it
from here—it looked so small!

The sky grew brighter as the sun rose.
Windrunner flew on steadily. Clover's eyelids

drooped, and he slept for a while. Ava held on to him, making sure he stayed safely on the dragon's back.

"I can see the unicorn herd," Windrunner growled, plunging downward.

The sky unicorns raised their heads as the storm dragon landed at the edge of their valley. One unicorn rushed forward, tossing her mane in delight.

Clover woke up and bounded down from the dragon's back to meet his mother again. They touched noses, and then Clover's mother nibbled his ear.

Ava and Sophy climbed down more slowly, and the herd of sky unicorns gathered round them.

"How strange that two girls and a storm dragon have brought our little Clover back to us," said one unicorn.

"Perhaps the stories from the songbirds are true," said another. "Can you talk to us, girls? Do you have magical stones that make this possible?"

"Yes, we do!" said Ava.

Both girls took out their stones and showed the sky unicorns the beautiful crystals inside. The magical animals nodded their heads and murmured to one another.

"I thank you for bringing my baby back to me," said Clover's mother, and she bowed her head to each of the girls and then to Windrunner. "I think the human who took him must be a very bad man."

Windrunner nodded his head, smoke billowing from his nostrils. "Sir Fitzroy is dangerous! What wicked ideas will he have next?"

"Then you haven't heard?" said Clover's mother. "The songbirds tell us he has sent letters to his friends across the kingdom, urging them to catch all magical animals. They say that there are already plans to catch the silver dolphins that live in the Great Ocean. A large boat with a giant net has been sent forth!"

Ava and Sophy exchanged looks.

"Then I'm going to find this boat and stop them!" cried Sophy.

"And I'll come with you!"
said Ava, lifting her chin. "We can't let Sir Fitzroy
win. We have to protect the silver dolphins."

A unicorn with a pale green tail stepped in
front of Ava. "My name is Marella," she said. "I
would like to repay the great help you have given
young Clover by offering to carry you anywhere
you wish to go."

"Thank you," said Ava, blushing. "I'd like that
very much!" She climbed onto Marella's back.

Clover bounced up to them. "Don't forget to come back and visit me, Ava!"

"I won't!" Ava beamed down at him. "I could never forget you, Clover!"

Sophy climbed onto Windrunner's back. The storm dragon and the sky unicorn soared side by side into the pale blue sky.

Ava smiled across at Sophy. She couldn't wait for their next secret rescue!

Don't miss another secret rescue!
A baby firebird is in trouble. Can Talia save it?